Max's Math

Kate Banks PICTURES BY Boris Kulikov

Frances Foster Books
Farrar Straus Giroux ■ New York

2+?=4
FBE♥2324

MAX had a problem.
He was building a car but he had only two wheels.
He needed four.
$2 + ? = 4$

Max went off to look for some wheels.
He found one in the basement
and another in the garage.
Now he had four wheels.
$2 + 2 = 4$
He could finish building the car.

Max started the car.
"Where are you going?" asked Max's brother Ben.
"To look for problems," said Max.
"Why would anyone go looking for problems?" asked Karl,
Max's other brother.
"Because it's fun," said Max.
"Can we come?" asked Karl.
"Sure," said Max.

For Pierluigi, whom I can always count on
—K.B.

For Frances
—B.K.

Farrar Straus Giroux Books for Young Readers
175 Fifth Avenue, New York 10010

Color separations by Bright Arts (H.K.) Ltd.
Printed in China by South China Printing Co. Ltd.,
Dongguan City, Guangdong Province
First edition, 2015
1 3 5 7 9 10 8 6 4 2

mackids.com

Library of Congress Cataloging-in-Publication Data
Banks, Kate, 1960–
Max's math / Kate Banks ; pictures by Boris Kulikov. — First edition.
pages cm
Summary: Max and his brothers drive to Shapeville and Count Town searching for problems, and are able to use their skills in arithmetic and sleuthing to help get things ready for a rocket launch.
ISBN 978-0-374-34875-5 (hardcover)
[1. Arithmetic—Fiction. 2. Numbers, Natural—Fiction. 3. Shape—Fiction.] I. Kulikov, Boris, 1966– illustrator. II. Title.
PZ7.B22594Maw 2015
[E]—dc23
2014015873

Farrar Straus Giroux Books for Young Readers may be purchased for business or promotional use. For information on bulk purchases please contact Macmillan Corporate and Premium Sales Department at (800) 221-7945 x5442 or by email at specialmarkets@macmillan.com.

1
7
9
2
3

Karl and Ben climbed into the car.
And off Max drove.

2+3+
+5=

He cruised down the highway past 10 vehicles:
2 buses, 3 trucks, and 5 motorcycles.

The road began to curve sharply.
"Stop!" cried Karl. "What's that?"
Max pulled over. An enormous number
lay in the grass.
"It's a 6," said Ben.
"Or a 9?" asked Karl.
"It's a mystery," said Max.
"We'd better take it with us," said Ben.

Max exited the highway.
To the left was Shapeville. To the right was Count Town.
"May I help you?" asked a traffic officer.
"We're looking for problems," said Max.
"There are plenty in either direction," said the officer.

FBE 2324

Max turned left and headed toward Shapeville.
The town was littered with triangles, circles, ovals, and other shapes of all sizes.
"We're looking for the town square," said Max to the mayor.
"You won't find it," said the mayor. "A storm passed through this morning and swept away all the squares. We don't have any left."

“No squares?” said Max. He parked the car.
Then he found two triangles in the rubble and put them together to make a square.
“Why, that’s extraordinary!” cried the mayor.
Soon all the townspeople were piecing together shapes.

Ben and Karl joined them.

Ben made a sign.

Karl made a kite.

But suddenly the kite began to rise and Karl went with it.
Max grabbed Karl's leg and followed.
Ben grabbed Max and soon they were floating aboveground.
They passed 5 clouds, 3 birds, and 1 airplane.
Then they drifted higher.
"Look at all the stars," said Ben.

"How are we going to get down?" asked Karl.
"Dot to dot," said Max.
He connected the stars, and in no time they were flying toward Shapeville.

"Watch out!" cried Ben. But it was too late.
They crashed through a clothesline,
scattering socks in all directions.
"Oh dear, my socks," cried a young man.
"Who will help me sort them?"
"We will," said Max.

Max and his brothers sorted the
socks into pairs and hung
them back on the clothesline.

The young man chose a fancy pair and put them on.
And just in time.
The citizens of Shapeville had lined up and were marching out of town.
"Where is everyone going?" asked Max.

“To Count Town,” said the mayor. “They are launching a rocket today.”
“I’d like to see that,” said Ben.
“Me too,” said Karl.
So Max and his brothers hopped into the car and followed the crowd.

But all was not well in Count Town.
Numbers were dashing here, there, and everywhere.
"What's going on?" asked Max.
"We have a problem," whispered someone. "A couple of numbers went missing during a game of hide-and-seek. We can't find number 0."
Max and his brothers set off to look for the 0.
They jumped onto a bench.

Karl spied a bird's nest with eggs.
Among them was the 0.
"Here it is," cried Karl.
"Oh, that's nothing," said the bird. "Let it be."
"It's not nothing," said Karl. "It's a zero. And without it there wouldn't be a 10."
"Or a 100," said Ben.
"Or a rocket launch," said Max. "Come on."

Max gave the zero a push, and it rolled out of the nest and got in line next to the number 1.

"We're ready for the countdown," said the mayor as everyone gathered at the launching site.

A large rocket was poised skyward.

"10 . . . 9 . . . 8 . . . 7 . . . " shouted the mayor.

But suddenly he stopped.

"Where is the 6?" he cried. "Hasn't anyone found it yet?"

Max opened the back of the car and took out the number 6.
"Here it is," he said. "It was hiding in the grass on the side of the road."
"Allow me to thank you," said the mayor.
He awarded Max and his brothers a golden ruler.

Then the countdown continued.
"6 . . . 5 . . . 4 . . . 3 . . . 2 . . . 1. Liftoff!" exclaimed the mayor.

And the rocket burst into the sky.

Afterward there was a celebration.
And Max and his brothers were invited.

The people of Shapeville provided the cake.
And the people of Count Town brought the ice cream.

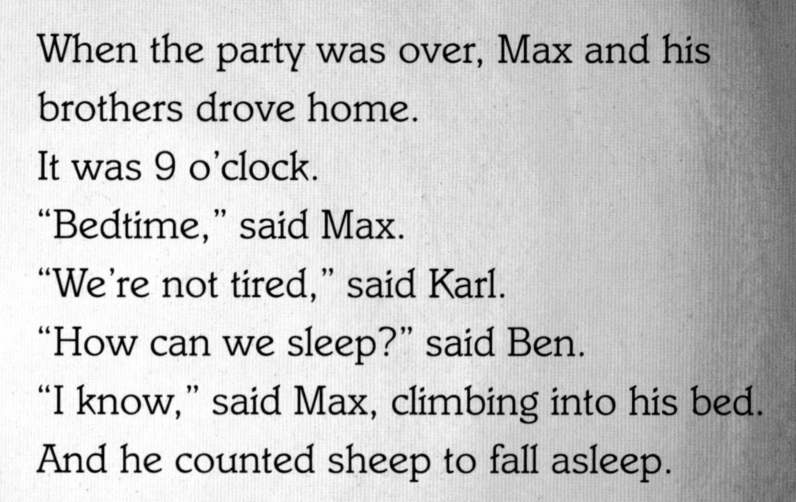

When the party was over, Max and his brothers drove home.
It was 9 o'clock.
"Bedtime," said Max.
"We're not tired," said Karl.
"How can we sleep?" said Ben.
"I know," said Max, climbing into his bed.
And he counted sheep to fall asleep.

7
4
1
5
3
6
0

6
5
4
0
8